Soul Looks Back in Wonder

SOUL

LOOKS BACK IN WONDER

TOM FEELINGS

PUFFIN BOOKS • New York

POEMS BY ▶

In
loving
memory of
JOHN OLIVER KILLENS
"a humble laborer with words"
who inspired us to follow his example
as a long-distance runner, warrior for the people

———————————————

Tom Feelings selected drawings of people he sketched while in Ghana and Senegal, West Africa;
Guyana, South America; as well as in the United States. He blueprinted his finished line drawings
onto sepia-toned sheets, and worked color into the figures with colored pencils. He then cut out
and cemented down various shapes in colored papers—textured, flat, plain, marbleized, as well as
wallpaper—to create the final overall collage effect. Some stencil cutouts were spray painted;
for instance, the art for which Haki R. Madhubuti composed "Destiny" was spray painted
on silver paper. This is the first book Tom Feelings has done in full color.

———————————————

PUFFIN BOOKS
Published by the Penguin Group
Penguin Putnam Books for Young Readers, 345 Hudson Street, New York, New York 10014, U.S.A.
Penguin Books Ltd, 27 Wrights Lane, London W8 5TZ, England
Penguin Books Australia Ltd, Ringwood, Victoria, Australia
Penguin Books Canada Ltd, 10 Alcorn Avenue, Toronto, Ontario, Canada M4V 3B2
Penguin Books (N.Z.) Ltd, 182-190 Wairau Road, Auckland 10, New Zealand

Penguin Books Ltd, Registered Offices: Harmondsworth, Middlesex, England

First published in the United States of America by Dial Books, a division of Penguin Books USA Inc., 1993
Published by Puffin Books, a member of Penguin Putnam Books for Young Readers, 1999

1 3 5 7 9 10 8 6 4 2

THE LIBRARY OF CONGRESS HAS CATALOGED THE DIAL EDITION AS FOLLOWS:
Soul looks back in wonder / [illustrated by] Tom Feelings;
poems by Maya Angelou . . . [et al.].
Summary: Artwork and poems by such writers as Maya Angelou, Langston Hughes, and Askia M. Touré
portray the creativity, strenght, and beauty of their African-American heritage.
ISBN 0-8037-1001-1
I. Feelings, Tom, ill. II. Angelou, Maya. III. Title.
PS591.N4S58 1993 811'.5080896073—dc20 93-824 CIP AC

Puffin Books ISBN 0-14-056501-9

Printed in the United States of America

"To You" © 1993 by the Estate of Langston Hughes
"window morning" © 1979 by Mwatabu Okantah. Originally published in *Nethula Journal*, Volume 1, Issue 1.
"Africa You Are Beautiful" © 1985 by Rashida Ismaili. Originally published as "Sur La Plage" by Shamal in *Onyibo*.
"Who Can Be Born Black" © 1981 by Mari Evans. Originally published in *Nightstar*, 1973–1978.
Quotation from *By Any Means Necessary* by Malcolm X © 1970, 1992 by Betty Shabazz and Pathfinder Press. Used by permission.

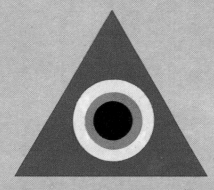

Today—the present—is a dangerous place for children of African descent, children of the sun. They are standing between childhood and adulthood, midway between the past and the future, pulled away from their center. They are removed from the benefits of ancient initiation rites—rites of passage designed to ease young people into manhood and womanhood, into the responsibilities and protection of full communal life. Too many teenagers are growing up in an environment where indifference and hostility are bullets aimed straight at the core of their spirits.

For four hundred years African creativity has been struggling to counter the narrow constraints of oppression, to circle it, turn it around, to seek order and meaning in the midst of chaos. My soul looks back in wonder at how African creativity has sustained us and how it still flows—seeking, searching for new ways to connect the ancient with the new, the young with the old, the unborn with the ancestors. Our creativity, moving, circling, improvising within the restricted form of oppression, reminds us that we must remain responsible to each other—we are not only individuals, but part of a collective that shares a common history and future. This book is a part of that flow of creativity.

The artists who came together to create *Soul Looks Back in Wonder* understand that one way to project our positive hopes for the future is for young people to see their own beauty reflected in our eyes, through our work. And so this book is for our precious young African sisters and brothers, who are our today and our tomorrow.

Tom Feelings

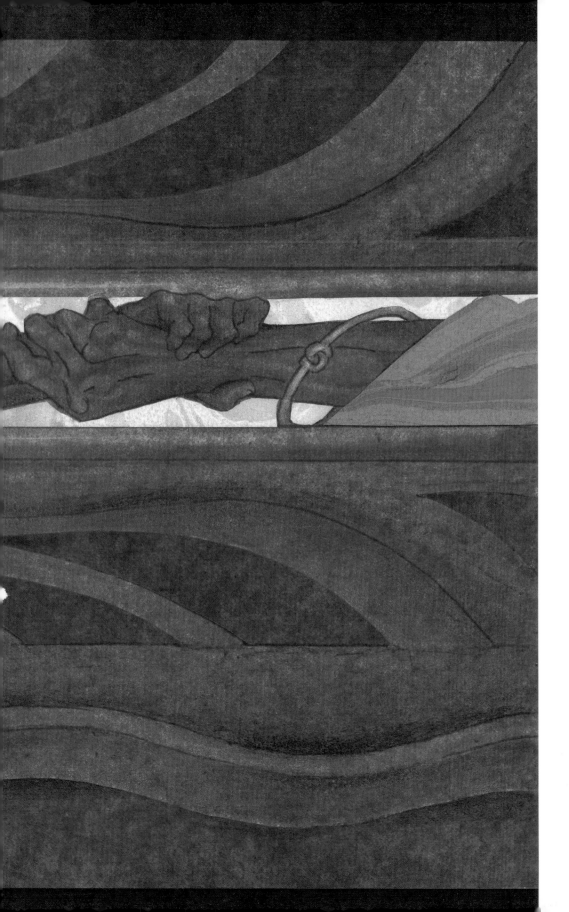

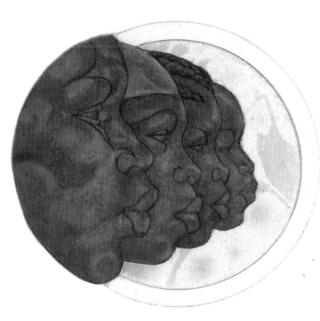

Mother of Brown-Ness

EARTH-MOTHER,
Mother of all our brown-ness,
Hands clasped with arms
    stretching round the world
Cuddle me closer, warm upon your breast
Slumberous, sweetly, darkness at rest.
Wake me to living and loving;
Scatter my dreams into the ethereal air.
Mother of brown-ness surround me
Deep in your sweet loving care.

Margaret Walker

Look at Us

look at us
we've grown into our eyes
often where we turn there are no trees
sometimes we dance to keep the winter out
sometimes we pose for self-esteem

what magic lies beneath the dust
what ancient fires darken our skin
to grow up where the sun is ice
the warmth lies deep within

Darryl Holmes

Boyz n Search of Their Soular System

Our boyz are short-fused in their short-changed Hood.
Yo, Gang-bangs reign where playgrounds grandly stood.
Shooters drive by: Teen-dreams dive for covers.
Nightmares stroke them like they were old lovers.
L.A.   Haiti   Kemet   Kingston—blues - groove:
Hip-hop/Gang-bang? Talk-slop/School-thang? Cool-move?
A swarm of conflict plagues their short-fused Hood.
Where Walking/death is forced to knock on Wood.

But Boyz must bond with Brothersblack, unbind
Their minds too roughly w/rapped in wondrous noise.
Though Black and short-fused in the fatal line.
Their Soular System gives them ancient poise.

Eugene B. Redmond

To You

To sit and dream, to sit and read,
To sit and learn about the world
Outside our world of here and now—
  Our problem world—
To dream of vast horizons of the soul
Through dreams made whole,
Unfettered, free—help me!
All you who are dreamers too,
    Help me to make
    Our world anew.
I reach out my dreams to you.

                    Langston Hughes

History of My People

My eyes touch, my fingers trace
The griot chants, clicks, songs of the Ancestors
The warrior words stretched taut across the soul
Drum words whispering the name of God
They say that beyond the blood-tide cries
    there is triumph
They say that beyond the blues-moan
    there is continuance
Triumph and continuance
A reaching back and a forward surge
A place where Black dreams swell consciousness
Even as the Niger swells old seasons into new life

        Walter Dean Myers

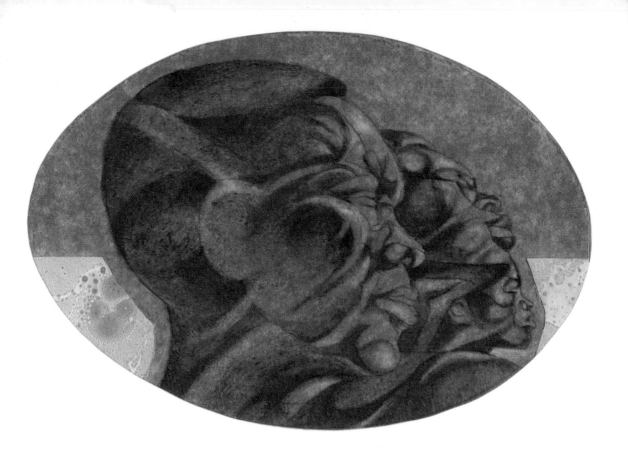

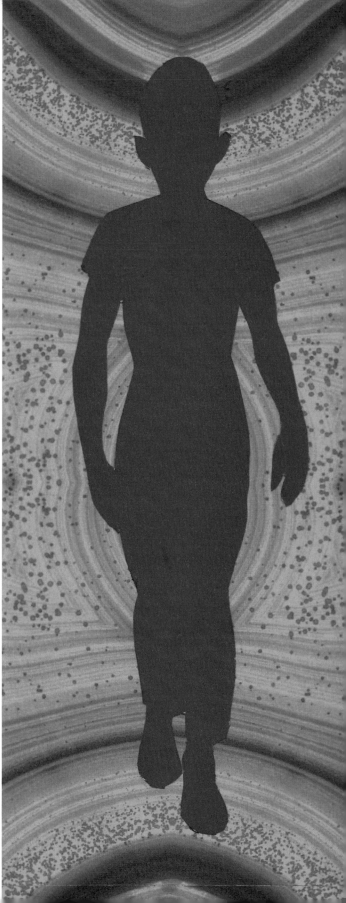

window morning

my ancestors
have claimed a storm
worn hollowed
tree
i am the wasteland
of our past
and at times
there is no air
yet i am a green bud

having broken
the earth womb
splitting the time
rooted trunk
of my beginning
my face
naked to God's sun

Mwatabu Okantah

Destiny

under volcanoes & timeless years within watch
and low tones. around corners, in deep caves among
misunderstood and sometimes meaningless sounds.
cut beggars, outlaw pimps & whores. resurrect work.
check your distance blue. come earthrise men
deepblack and ready, come sunbaked women rootculture on the move.
just do what you're supposed to do, what you say you gonta do
not the impossible, not the unimaginative,
not copy clothed as original and surely
not bitter songs in european melodies. take hold
do the necessary, the possible, the correctly simple
talk of missions & interpret destiny
put land and selfhood on the minds of our people
do the expected, do what all people do
reverse destruction. capture tomorrows.

Haki R. Madhubuti

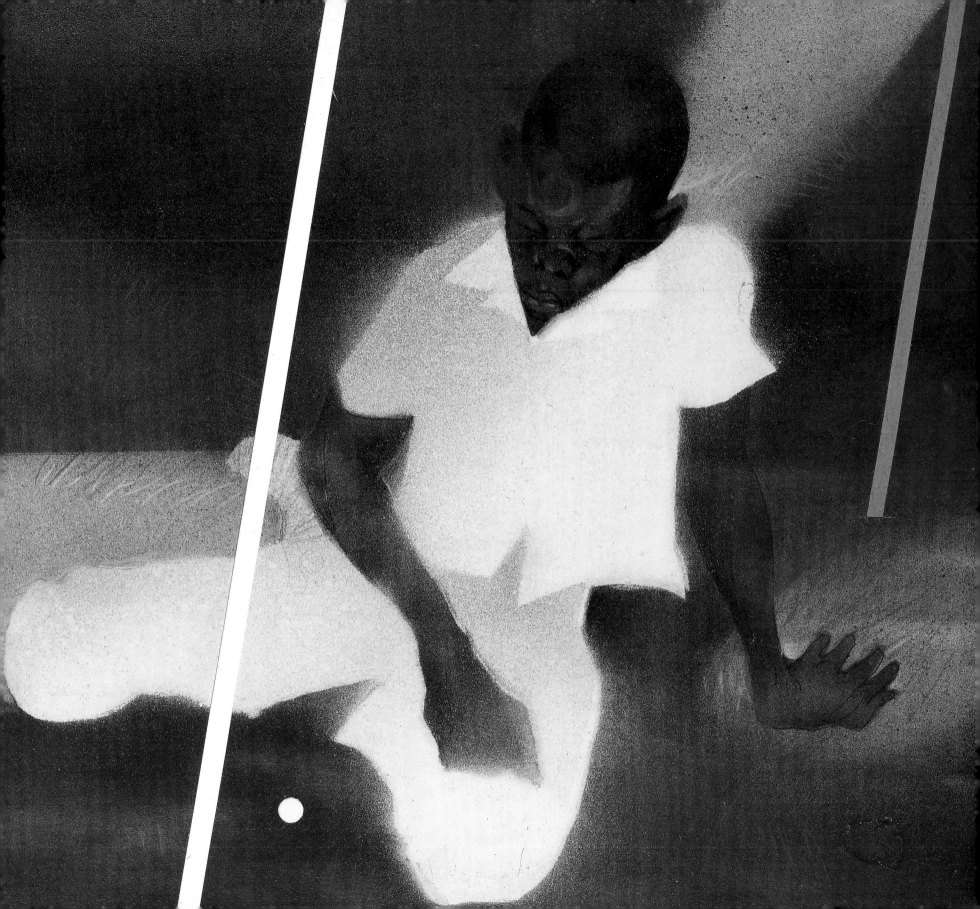

I Love the Look of Words

Popcorn leaps, popping from the floor
of a hot black skillet
and into my mouth.
Black words leap,
snapping from the white
page. Rushing into my eyes. Sliding
into my brain which gobbles them
the way my tongue and teeth
chomp the buttered popcorn.

When I have stopped reading,
ideas from the words stay stuck
in my mind, like the sweet
smell of butter perfuming my
fingers long after the popcorn
is finished.

I love the book and the look of words
the weight of ideas that popped into my mind
I love the tracks
of new thinking in my mind.

Maya Angelou

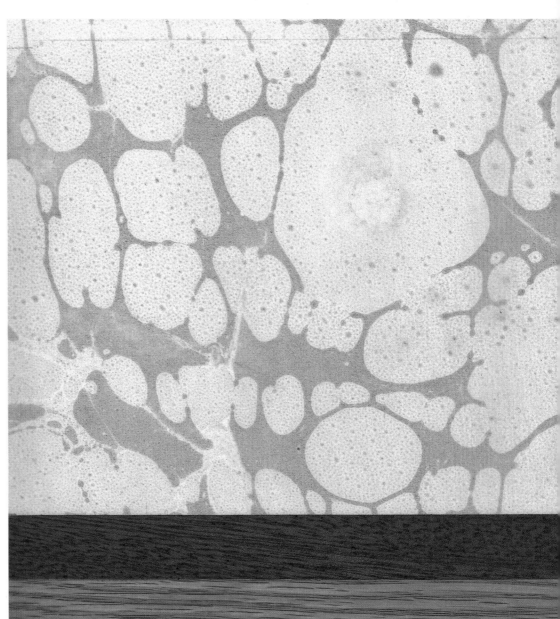

Africa You Are Beautiful

Has anyone told you
      You are beautiful
Africa?
      Your full body
and sensuous lips
      have kissed my soul
and Africa, I am bound to You
      by the drumbeat of
my heart that pumps the
      blood of my birthright
and You are mine.

Rashidah Ismaili

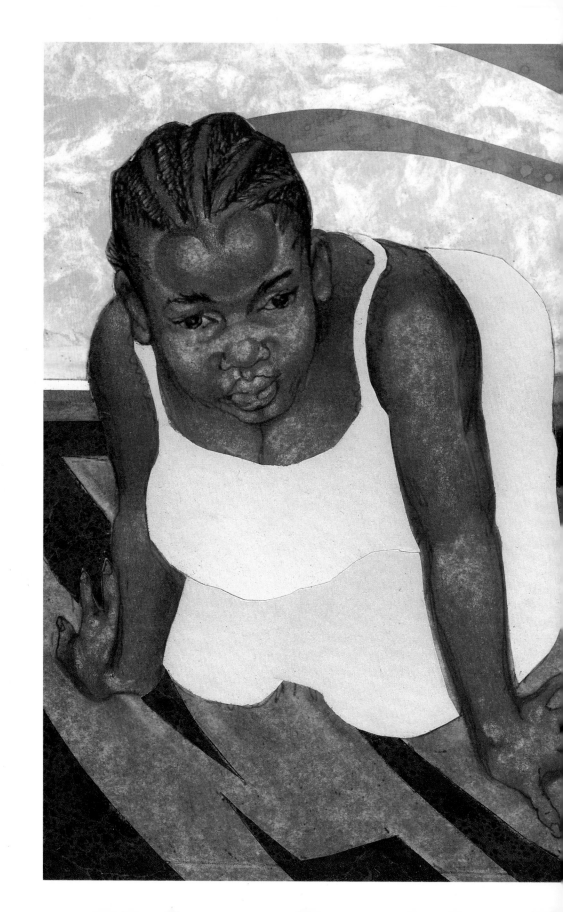

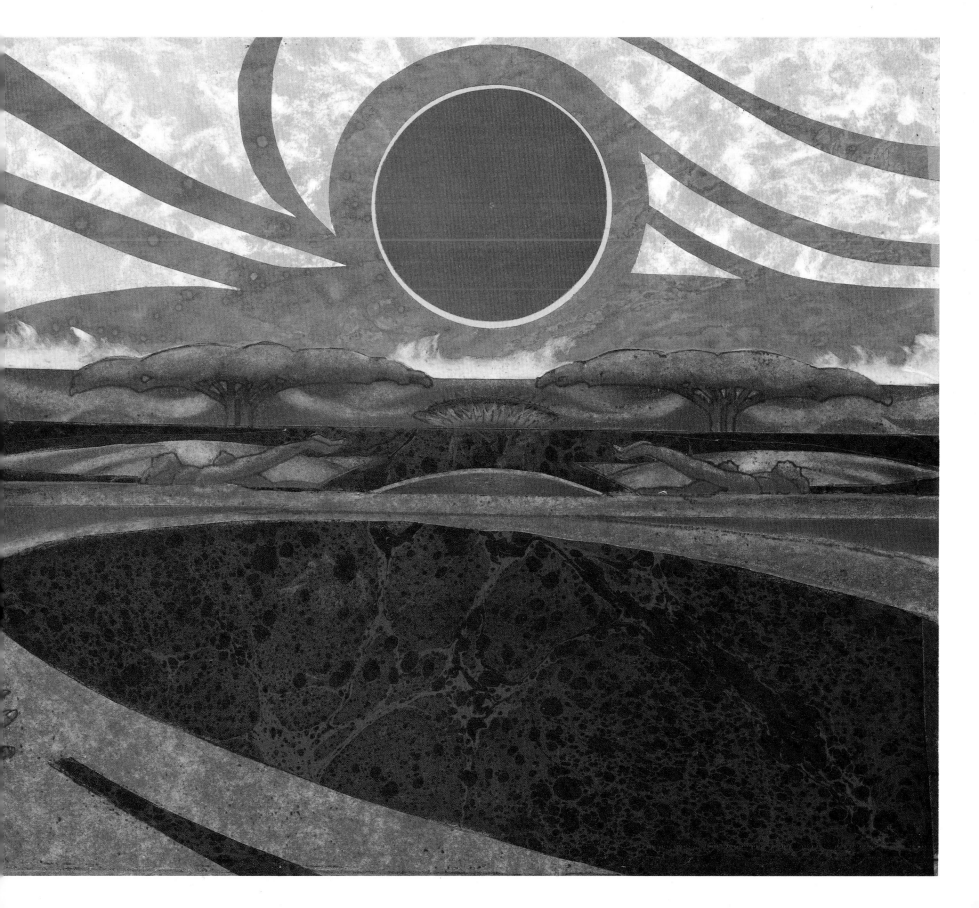

Rhythms, Harmonies, Ancestors
(A Spirit Rap)

To be instantly alive, feeling the vibes
of Time's magical rhythms; a young, Black man
breathing pure air, beneath Heaven's endless blue.
Here nature itself is colorful, warm, but dangerous,
like me; or a def jam: Souljah or X-Clan walking
the land with great, Ancestor smiles. Or in close
harmony, rowing the Nile, parting the Sea,
seven brothers pulling swiftly, hot sun burning
beauty, loving strength into our sweaty backs;
a thousand Harambees sing in our tropical minds!

Askia M. Touré

I am the creativity

I am the dance step
of the paintbrush singing
I am the sculpture
of the song
the flame breath
of words
giving new life to paper
yes, I am the creativity
that never dies
I am the creativity
keeping my people
alive

Alexis De Veaux

Under the Rainbow

I close my eyes
and slide along the arc
to home where my long grandmothers
sleep, dreaming of me,
dreaming of how dark
and beautiful we are together
under the bright
rainbow of our nights.

Lucille Clifton

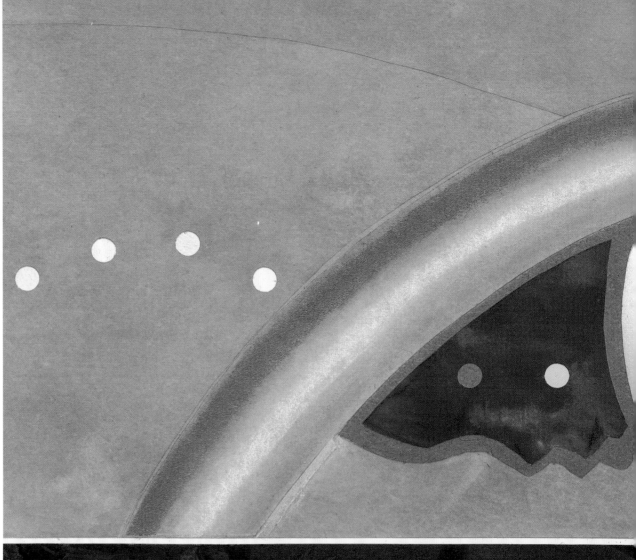

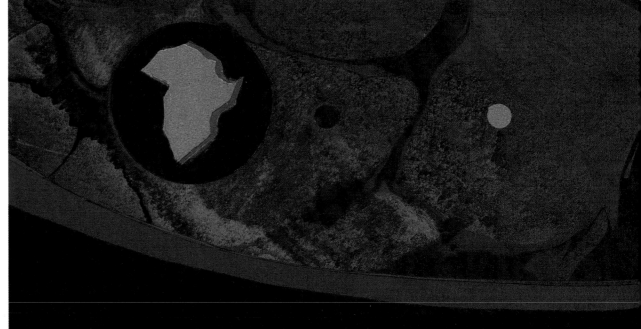

Who Can
Be Born Black

Who
can be born black
and not
sing
the wonder of it
the joy
the
challenge

And/to come together
in a coming togetherness
vibrating with the fires of pure knowing
reeling with power
ringing with the sound above sound
     above sound
to explode/in the majesty of our oneness
our comingtogether
in a comingtogetherness

Who
can be born
black
and not exult!

Mari Evans

MARGARET WALKER grew up in Alabama and Mississippi, where she heard family stories about her great-grandmother who was caught and flogged while fleeing slavery. In *Jubilee* Dr. Walker wrote about her great-grandmother's life and her goal to obtain freedom and education for her children. Dr. Walker's poem sets the tone for *Soul* with a message of collective responsibility. An award-winning poet and author, Dr. Walker taught at Jackson State College and now resides in Jackson, Mississippi.

DARRYL HOLMES, the youngest poet writing for *Soul*, is from Brooklyn, New York. A graduate of Queens College, he is obtaining a Master of Fine Arts degree at Brooklyn College while working at an insurance company, as Wallace Stevens did. He enjoys writing for young people because they are "unafraid to put their hearts on the line."

EUGENE B. REDMOND was born in St. Louis, Missouri, and raised in East St. Louis, Illinois, on the Mississippi, where he swam, fished, boated, and listened to stories. He remembers his excitement when his heroes, Jacob and Benjamin in the Bible, as well as Captain Marvel and Superman, seemed to come to life in the person of Jomo Kenyatta, who ruled Kenya after its independence from British colonial rule. Professor Redmond, who teaches English at Southern Illinois University at Edwardsville, has also taught poetry for many years in the East St. Louis schools.

LANGSTON HUGHES, born in 1902 in Joplin, Missouri, is one of the giants of twentieth-century literature. While working in a restaurant in Washington, D.C., he gave three poems to poet Vachel Lindsay, who reported his discovery of a major new poet to newspapers across the country. "To You" was composed by Langston Hughes to accompany Tom Feelings's art on a poster for the Congress of Racial Equality in 1962, and it is here published for the first time. At the time of his death in New York City in 1967, Mr. Hughes had twenty-seven books in print.

WALTER DEAN MYERS, born in Martinsburg, West Virginia, remembers writing his first poem in fifth grade in Harlem. Growing up he liked basketball, recess, and junk food, but he loved books because he could explore worlds both outside and inside himself. A prize-winning author with two Newbery Honor Awards and four Coretta Scott King Awards, he has over twenty books in print. He lives in Jersey City, New Jersey.

MWATABU OKANTAH, born in Orange, New Jersey, frequently performs his work with musicians, since he feels poetry is about *listening*. He likes audiences with young people because "poetry is still alive in them. They represent our real possibility." He is Professor of Pan-African Studies at Kent State University in Ohio.

HAKI R. MADHUBUTI, poet and teacher, publisher and entrepreneur, started Third World Press in Chicago in 1967 with two friends and a mimeograph machine. His company has hundreds of books in print, and he received the American Book Award for his contribution to publishing in 1991. He also teaches at Chicago State University. He learned from Langston Hughes never to lose an opportunity to fulfill his dream, so after his poetry readings he sells his books.

MAYA ANGELOU was born in St. Louis and grew up in Stamps, Arkansas. She recalls her grandmother's friend Mrs. Flowers, who read poetry and fiction aloud to her: "Most of the things I do now come out of what that understanding woman read to me and got me to reading as a child." An award-winning and best-selling author and poet, Ms. Angelou composed and read a poem at President Clinton's 1993 inauguration. She teaches at Wake Forest University in Winston-Salem, North Carolina.

RASHIDAH ISMAILI was born in Dahomey and lived in Nigeria before moving to New York City. She wrote her first story when she was eight and delighted in her imagined world. As a single parent in New York City she raised her son imparting the strength and serenity of his African heritage. She is the Associate Director of the Higher Education Opportunity Program at Pratt Institute in Brooklyn, New York.

ASKIA M. TOURÉ was born in Raleigh, North Carolina, and grew up in Dayton, Ohio. In 1968 he pioneered the teaching of African-American Studies in the U.S. at San Francisco State University. He won the American Book Award for *From the Pyramids to the Projects* in 1989. He lives in Atlanta, Georgia, where he writes and makes time to work with a rap group.

ALEXIS DE VEAUX, born in New York City, writes for young people because "this is their world and I want them to own it." Learning is a brightly burning passion for her, since she never forgets it was once illegal for Black people to learn to read and write. She completed her doctorate at State University of New York-Buffalo where she now teaches American Studies.

LUCILLE CLIFTON grew up in Depew, New York, now lives in Columbia, Maryland, and teaches poetry at St. Mary's College. As a youngster she adored reading: "Both my parents read books all the time. The love of words was very natural to me, and I grew up reading everything I could get my hands on. I was one of those cereal box readers." Winner of the Coretta Scott King Award, her stories are often inspired by the activities of her six children and five grandchildren.

MARI EVANS is a writer, activist, and musician in Indianapolis, Indiana. Her closing poem is a clear statement of the common destiny of Black people and a powerful celebration of Africanity.

Education is an important element in the struggle for human rights.
It is the means to help our children and people rediscover their identity and
thereby increase self-respect. Education is our passport to the future,
for tomorrow belongs to the people who prepare for it today.

MALCOLM X